W9-BWT-214

SNOWY FARM

Calvin Shaw

*

illustrated by
Oamul Lu

A Paula Wiseman Book
Simon & Schuster Books for Young Readers
New York London Toronto Sydney New Delhi

There's a snowy white windmill
on a snowy white farm,
with a frosty old house
and a snow-covered barn.

With bundled-up horses
and bundled-up hens
and icicle carrots
for our bundled-up friends.

They're living on ice
with no grass at hand.

They're living on water
more than living on land.

With ripe snowball apples,
the farmer is fed
as he rides along
on a big tractor sled.

While working the fields
in their warm winter coats,
snow angels are made
by the chickens and goats.

The mom of the family
is cooking a dish
with savory spices
and seasonal fish.

Outside of her window,
her kids work the field.
The chickens are fed
and the apples are peeled.

The dinner bell rings,
and the doors open wide.

With snowballs aplenty,
the kids run inside.

They help set the table,
and feast in delight,
a family together
on a cold winter night.

When supper is finished
they sit by the fire.

The warmth of
their loved ones
is all they desire.

Yawning and dozing,
they all say, "Good night."
Slipping into their beds . . .

they're all tucked in tight.

With starlight appearing,
they're warm and at ease,
while falling asleep
to a cold winter breeze.

Now everyone's dreaming
in snowy white charm . . .

and everything's peaceful
at last on the farm.

Author's Note

When I began writing *Snowy Farm* years ago, I would jot down ideas in a notepad that included icicle carrots, snowball apples, and tractor sleds. As time passed, I would try to get more ideas for the story by researching the coldest and snowiest regions of the world.

The coldest place on Earth is Antarctica. Antarctica is one of Earth's seven continents. It is covered by a massive sheet of ice approximately 9,000 feet thick. Temperatures can fall as low as -135 degrees Fahrenheit. The peak summer months of Antarctica are December, January, and February. During this time, Antarctica is tilted toward the sun, and daylight lasts for twenty-four hours. In the peak winter months of June, July, and August, Antarctica is tilted away from the sun, and there is no daylight.

The people who travel to or live in Antarctica fall into two main groups, those who live and work on scientific research stations or bases, and tourists. No one lives in Antarctica indefinitely in the way that people do in the rest of the world. Antarctica has no commercial industries, no towns or cities, no permanent residents.

I have not traveled to Antarctica myself, but I hope to one day. Until then, this book can be our imagined journey there together.

For Mom, Dad, and Duncan
–C. S.

For my nephew–enjoy your childhood
–O. L.

SIMON & SCHUSTER BOOKS FOR YOUNG READERS
An imprint of Simon & Schuster Children's Publishing Division
1230 Avenue of the Americas, New York, New York 10020

For information about special discounts for bulk purchases, please contact Simon & Schuster
Special Sales at 1-866-506-1949 or business@simonandschuster.com.
The Simon & Schuster Speakers Bureau can bring authors to your live event.
For more information or to book an event, contact the Simon & Schuster Speakers
Bureau at 1-866-248-3049 or visit our website at www.simonspeakers.com.
Book design by Ann Bobco
The text for this book was set in Aged Book.
The illustrations for this book were rendered digitally.
Manufactured in China
0819 SCP
First Edition
10 9 8 7 6 5 4 3 2 1
Library of Congress Cataloging-in-Publication Data
Names: Shaw, Calvin, author. | Lu, Oamul, illustrator.
Title: Snowy farm / Calvin Shaw ; illustrated by Oamul Lu.
Description: First edition. | New York : Simon & Schuster Books for Young Readers, [2019] |
"A Paula Wiseman Book." | Summary: Illustrations and simple, rhyming text portray a
family living on a farm with a snowy white house and barn, bundled-up horses
and hens, and all they can possibly need.
Identifiers: LCCN 2017061225 | ISBN 9781534410473 (hardcover) | ISBN 9781534410480 (eBook)
Subjects: | CYAC: Stories in rhyme. | Farm life–Arctic regions–Fiction. | Arctic regions–Fiction.
Classification: LCC PZ8.3.S53248 Igl 2018 | DDC [E]–dc23
LC record available at https://lccn.loc.gov/2017061225